Ooh Yes I Woof!

written by Richard Gough-Buijs

'Ooh Yes I Woof!' The adventures of a Miniature Schnauzer

written by Richard Gough-Buijs.

illustrations by Richard Gough-Buijs.

Copyright © 2016 by Richard Gough-Buijs.

Cover design & book design by Richard Gough-Buijs.

Contact: richardgoughbuijs@icloud.com

You can follow or like 'Ooh Yes I Woof The adventures of a Miniature Schnauzer' on Twitter and Facebook.

First Printing: 2016
Publisher: CreateSpace

ISBN-13: 978-1507745847
ISBN-10: 1507745842

The adventures of a Miniature Schnauzer

Ooh Yes I Woof!

written by Richard Gough-Buijs

If I could have a child,

with the ears of a rabbit,

with eyes in the shape of almonds,

with fur that is white like snow,

and as black as the night,

with big bushy eyebrows, a beard and a moustache,

as bouncy as a kangaroo,

as growly as a bear,

as clever as Sherlock,

and a big personality.

It would be a ...
black and silver Miniature Schnauzer

Index

Dear reader

Once upon a time, during the winter of 1970, a boy named Richard was born in The Netherlands. His father worked for a Dutch coffee company and in his spare-time he watched football and cycling. He also enjoyed doing carpentry in the attic.
Richard's mother was a domestic house goddess and also helped out her own mother and neighbour with house cleaning. She loved cycling and sang along to songs from Neil Diamond to Barbra Streisand.

Two years and four months later there was a huge storm and a stork brought a little baby brother to their family home who was nicknamed Koko. His brother Koko liked pulling faces and he enjoyed eating his meals with apple puree.

Richard loved to clean the house with grandmother's vacuum cleaner and he loved listening to music. On one of his birthdays he was given a vinyl album by ABBA and the song 'Dancing Queen' became one of his most favourite songs.

Many years later Richard moved to Brighton where he met his future husband Michael at a Eurovision Song Contest party organised by their friends David and Declan. Michael likes traveling, singing and eating Charbonnel et Walker's pink Marc de Champagne truffles. They both married in a palace, the Royal Pavilion in Brighton and lived happily ever after.

Nowadays Richard cleans their house with a Dyson hoover and he listens to ABBA music on iTunes.

The music from ABBA has played an important role in my life. I don't know if you've heard about them but they became one of the most popular music bands in the world after they won the Eurovision Song Contest in the Royal Pavilion in Brighton.
You may have heard their songs on the radio or listened to them online or perhaps you have seen the musical or the film 'Mamma Mia'.

Michael & I wedded in the Royal Pavilion in 2011 where ABBA won the contest and the day was celebrated with our family and friends. It is still the most beautiful day of my life. We always wanted to expand our family and for many years we have been talking about getting a dog. A fluffy creature that could sit on your lap whilst reading a book or watching a film, or laying next to you on the sofa being stroked and cuddled. A little furry animal that would be sweet and obedient at all times. Wouldn't it be great to take your little pooch out for a nice and long walk in the country side on a lovely sunny Summer day? The perfect life of a married couple and their dog. Every time when we spoke about it we were getting more and more excited and it was a just a matter of how to fit a dog into our busy lives.

We ultimately agreed that we would like to get a Miniature Schnauzer. The breed looks a little bit like the dog Snowy in the Tin Tin comics series by Hergé and sometimes it reminds me a little bit of Muttley, the animated fictional character created by Hanna-Barbera. I always wondered whether they were Miniature Schnauzers. It's amazing that we've got internet where you can instantly get an answer to your questions. According to the search results Snowy was a white wire-haired fox terrier and Muttley appeared to be a mixed breed dog.

All dogs look amazing (and beautiful) but according to me you can't beat the looks of a Miniature Schnauzer. They look grumpy, they have a massive moustache and beard and they are also famous for their very noticeable eye brows! It would be a dog that you could easily show off to other people.

We bought a reference book about Miniature Schnauzers and a general puppy-training book. You do learn a lot from those books and it gave a lot of insight in the breed's needs, do's and don'ts and all the tricks they can learn.

We didn't realise it at first but the more we read about the Miniature Schnauzers the more we realised that they need a lot of attention and most of all: company. For example, the book stated that you can only leave them alone for up to 3 or 4 hours should you need to go away. Both of us were working, we had a big social life and we loved going on holidays.

The main question was: how would we adjust our lifestyle? When you bring a puppy into your household you make the commitment to care for them, feed them, play with them, walk them and love them!

I was convinced that raising a dog would be a very easy task. According to me, within two weeks the dog would be potty trained and after that we would be concentrating on learning the doggy how to sit, stay, wait and lay down. Our dog would be a perfect dog in no time. We also planned we would have a dog-sitter coming around over lunch whilst we were at work. We would be looking after the dog during the mornings, late afternoons into the evenings and over the weekends. It was easy peasy and we would be living happily ever after.

I had read in the books that Miniature Schnauzers are known for being playful and vocal. They adore company and they love to be out and about. They are constantly on their guard and will make owners aware when there's some unusual things happening in or around the house.

It was the year 2014 in which we decided to go for it. Let's get a Miniature Schnauzer. It's going to be great fun!

Two significant events happened during 2014: the Prime Minister and the Queen introduced a new law that made it possible for boys to marry boys and for girls to marry girls in the UK. The second significant event was that I got officially married! Michael and I wedded in 2011 and our wedding was called a civil partnership at that time. So it happened that we made an appointment with the town hall in Brighton to change our partnership over into a marriage.

On that special day we brought a very special witness along to Brighton Town Hall, our black and silver Miniature Schnauzer called Buster! We tried to keep it a secret from the press but when our witness arrived at Bartholomew Square he was welcomed by thousands of people. From the moment he put his paws onto the red carpet people were cheering and calling his name.

People took lots of selfies with Buster and many admirers had their arms and faces 'signed' with muddy paw-prints from Buster. There were cameras everywhere with bright dazzling flashing lights. The journalists, holding their note pads and voice recorders, were trying to attract his attention for an interview and the crowds were shouting his name.

The atmosphere was ecstatic! He is handsome, he is cute, very distinguished and he loves attention! I bet you are eager to find out everything about this beautiful boy!

Let's start at the very beginning of this book. A story about fun, love, making friends and sometimes a scary moment.

Enjoy the adventures of a Miniature Schnauzer!

Richard

It's a boy!

On a beautiful sunny day in July Daddy Michael and Daddy Richard were watching a film at their home. Suddenly they were interrupted by 'a massive explosion' which left them trembling. A pelican had fallen through the roof of the conservatory and it had very gently dropped a little cloth bundle onto the floor.

Until now it was believed that a stork can be seen flying over rooftops with a little cloth bundle before landing at the doorstep of a happy couple who then unwrap their smiling newborn. Once upon a time this was a common story to tell children who were deemed too young to be told anything different.
It's not a natural phenomenon that pelicans fall through roofs, especially when they carry a tiny little bundle. However, the pelican may have been blinded by the flashing lights of a satellite, disorientated by the wireless internet connection or it simply overlooked the chimney on the top of the roof. We will never know.

Luckily the bird and the little newborn were unharmed. You may think this sort of thing is a myth but when you see the damage to the roof, with a print of a massive bird with its wings spread out wide, you realise it is not. Luckily the weather was warm and dry but what would happen if it started to rain? The conservatory would be totally flooded. That would be a panic! The roof needed to be repaired as a matter of urgency. Especially when you live in the UK where rain showers can prove to be torrential.

" I'm sorry but can I get your attention please! Who really cares about the roof?" The voice appeared to come from the little cloth bundle. Michael and Richard walked to the bundle and started to unwrap it. "Oi, can we be a little bit more careful please? Thank you". Blimey, there was one feisty little thing inside of it. The last layer of the bundle was now about to be unfolded and there he was ... it's a boy!
The young little wonder. He was smiling and he was making little squeaky noises. He liked his new house. He liked his daddies. Michael & Richard took the boy-wonder out of the cloth bundle and gave him lots of cuddles. They lifted him up towards the sky. Four hands were holding up a puppy-dog to the sky in front of a big dazzling sun.

The Baron and Baroness of Windlesham

"I was born in the picturesque village of 'Windlesham'. This lovely village is situated in the borough of Surrey in the South of England. Its name derived from the river Windle Brook which runs south of the village into Chobham and the common suffix 'ham' is the Old English word for a farmhouse.

Thousands and thousands of years ago 'Windlesham' belonged to mythological creatures who lived in the enchanted forest. Amongst the creatures were playful gnomes, dancing elves and fairies, galloping fauns, singing goblins, howling nymphs and ugly mini-trolls. They parachuted down from dandelions, jumped from one flower to another, ran over branches and bark. They would have very long naps on the mushrooms and they loved playing around with the butterflies, the animals and the birds.
Today the forest still exists and it's a place full of mystery with Scots Pines, areas of mixed broad-leaved woodland including twelve old oak trees, several Silver Birches and Sweet Chestnut trees where you can let your imagination run free.
The mythological creatures still live there. I have seen them, I swear! Always keep an eye out for them and I'll keep my ears wide open.

I was born at the manor of Baron Ian Bark and Baroness Ida Bark situated in the beautiful forestial surroundings of Windlesham. Baroness Bark was a social creature and absolutely adored socialising with her relatives, friends and acquaintances. Quite often she organised afternoon tea parties at the gilded Indian pavilion in the forest where not only the tea but also wine and bubbly would flow. Her chocolatiers, patisserie makers, cake decorators and bakers created the most sumptuous and delicious truffles, macaroons, victorian sponges and sandwiches. The scones were served with home made marmalade and the most scrumptious clotted cream you could ever dream of! Yum! I am not sure who could have ever exceeded Mrs Bark's Afternoon Tea parties. Perhaps the Queen's Afternoon Tea Parties in Buckingham Palace? Oh I would love to have been invited to one of Her Royal Majesty's tea parties. Dream, dream, dream.
When I lived at the manor I remember that Baron Ian always used to wear freshly ironed white clothes that smelled of lavender. Every time when I saw the Baron he was playing golf in the house. Baron Ian would play golf in every room.

He was obviously very careful in the rooms which were full of the most expensive and exclusive furniture, rare ornaments and the most extraordinary statues.

Baron Ian was an excellent golf player and on the odd occasion one of the white balls would go missing. He had looked under the oak chairs, the chest of draws, the art-deco saloon table and the coffee table but not a sign of the golf balls. He had looked behind the velvet curtains, underneath the runners in the hallway and under the Persian carpets but he couldn't find any of the missing balls. The Barks hired a team of golf-ball detectors, they had a seance where they tried to made contact with the balls in case they had gone over to the other side and they even had all the furniture removed and the floors ripped out in order to find the balls. Unfortunately there was no sign of the balls. It remained one of the biggest mysteries and Mr and Mrs Bark were completely baffled by it.

It wasn't until my Miniature Schnauzer uncle called Rover was feeling a little bit under the weather. Mr and Mrs Bark tried to perk him up but all he wanted to do was to lie down and sleep. This was extraordinary and my uncle was taken to the animal doctor where the staff took an X-ray. The Baron and the Baroness were seated in the waiting room. They were both very nervous. It only took ten minutes for the results to come through. The X-Ray showed that uncle Rover had round objects in his stomach! Uncle Rover had not four, nor five or six but seven golf balls in his tummy! That was an awful lot for a dog. Roar! The animal doctor removed the balls straight away and uncle Rover made a speedy recovery. Both the Baron and the Baroness were over the moon and uncle Rover was 'happy as Larry' again. Baron Ian promised that he would never ever play golf in the house again.

The Baron and the Baroness had a lot of Miniature Schnauzers living at their home. One of their Miniature Schnauzers was my mother, a very beautiful and pretty dog. On a sunny day she met my father, who had a very waggly black tail. They really liked each other and shortly there after, me, my brothers and sister were born. We lived at the rear of the Bark's beautiful manor house and we had our own residence with a big play-ground where I could run around and play with my siblings.I loved it!

There was sunshine every day and it was nice and warm. Everyday we played with each other and we ran around in circles until I was so tired that I had to go to sleep.

Sleeping is one of may favourite things to do but I can't wait to wake up so I can start to play again. Playing is one of my favourite things to do. I've got many favourite things like eating, drinking, running, chewing, barking. Every kind of activity is my favourite thing to do. But you can always wake me up for a play!

On a very hot day during the Summer the Baroness noticed that her feet were swollen. The humidity in the air was high but the baroness didn't want to pay too much attention to it. The following day the baroness was woken up by a knock on the door of the bedroom. Her servant brought the baroness a pair of her slippers. She put them on and got out of the bed. But ... something wasn't right. She noticed that there was something unusual about her slippers. An odd feeling. She looked down to the slippers and noticed that they were too small for her feet. She asked her servant to bring in another pair. A few minutes later she put the second pair on but again the slippers were too small. It could have been the case that all pairs of slippers have shrunken overnight or it could be the case that the baroness's feet had grown bigger!

Ten minutes later the air was filled with the sounds of ambulance sirens. Shortly thereafter the paramedics stormed through the front gates of the manor and came to take the baroness to the hospital. When the ambulance drove off they put the sirens back on. Upon hearing the loud sirens I decided to throw my head into the air and I started to howl along to the sound of the sirens.

Every week the Baroness stayed in the hospital from Monday until Friday until her feet were back to their normal size again. Friday afternoon she would return to the manor where she would walk through the house and the forest in her best slippers. During the weekend she would wear every pair of slippers she had. By Sunday evening her feet had grown bigger again and she was using walking sticks, zimmer-frames and even wheelchairs to move herself around. Every Monday morning the ambulance with the sirens would take her back to the hospital again. Every time when I hear the sirens of an emergency service vehicle I will howl. I think there's a pack of wolves hiding inside them. It sounds like they make them howl and then they amplify their sounds. But I can even howl louder than they do. Ha! I can howl! Hell yeah!

The truth is that I slept quite often during my life at the Bark's Manor House and their large surrounding forest. I love sleeping. Have I told you it's one of my most favourite things? My brothers and sister were most often asleep too.

Beside sleeping I like playing too! I did play quite a bit with the older miniature schnauzers who were around. One of them was my grand mother.

My granny was called Jess and she was definitely one of the most influential Miniature Schnauzer in the country. My granny was famous for the highest jump ever and for winning the 60 meters hurdles. A true champion! I also loved to run around the Tea Pavilion with my father Mo-Ja. We used to run miles and miles through the forest chasing the birds and the rabbits. We would jump over branches and ran around very fast. Run! Run! Run! My father is world champion runner for winning the 5,000 and 10,000 meters! I've inherited that skill and one day I'm going to show that to the rest of the world.

The Baroness was only at the manor over the weekends and I met a lot of exciting people who came down to see the baroness for afternoon tea parties. They loved playing with me and I thoroughly enjoyed it. Exciting times! The Baron sporadically made an appearance during those parties and most often he would be playing croquet in the fields.

The Baron and Baroness found it a challenge to look after the Miniature Schnauzers due to their health issues and old age so they decided to find each and everyone of us a new home.

Daddy Michael
and
Daddy Richard

On a beautiful sunny day two bearded men in a vroom-vroom arrived at the Manor House. They drove up from down South near Brighton and ... they came to visit me! Take me away, take me away! Yes! Yes! Yes! Now!

They played with me, they stroked me, they lifted me up and they took loads of pictures of me! They were telling Ida, the Baroness, that they would be going on holiday to an island called Mykonos in the Aegean Sea and they would love to come back to the Baron and Baroness to collect me upon their return. I was a very happy doggy! A new home!

Two men with moustaches and beards and the box on wheels would come to collect me within one month! Yes!

I only had a few weeks left at the beautiful manor house with its stunning forests. I would make the most of this time and I could still be running around with granny Jess and daddy Mo-Ja. But very soon I would be going down South.

The city life, the beach, the white cliffs and the South Downs. Eating and drinking in the Shepherd & Dog and the Hare & Hounds. Din dins in restaurant the Ginger Dog and Sunday Roasts in the Camelford Arms. Then a bit of chilling-out at Chubby Chops in Hove.

At home I would be on sentry-duty like the guards of Buckingham Palace. I would alert my daddies when the postman would deliver the post, I would make them aware when the Waitrose deliverer had arrived and I would let them know when somebody was passing by our home. Obviously my senses would be on high alert when an emergency service vehicle was approaching. I can't wait to live in my new home!

I'm ready! Take me now pelican and bring me over to Brighton! I'll be starting a new life with my two bearded daddies with my new name Buster!

A Giant Schnauzer

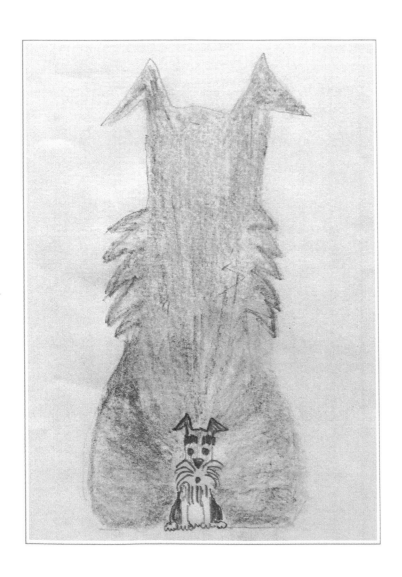

My name is Buster. I am a black and silver Giant Schnauzer and I'm living with my Daddy Michael and Daddy Richard. Actually, I am super hero Giant Schnauzer. I am also related to the growling bears, bouncy kangaroos and the forever sniffing rabbits.

When people ask my daddies what kind of breed I am they keep on telling them that I am a Miniature Schnauzer. I hear this day in and day out wherever we are. Whether it is on the streets, at the white cliffs or in the Downs. They've got completely the wrong end of the stick.

People always say that I have big ears and a big moustache. There you are. You see? That proves I am a giant dog! Why can't they understand that I am the tallest and biggest dog in the world?

When I growl I do sound like a bear, and if I want I can roar like a very noisy grizzly bear. RRRROOOOAAAAARRRRRRRR!!!

I think it's unnecessary to prove it to you but have I mentioned yet that I can bark? Every neighbour and post deliverer will be able to tell you.

Let me tell you that I got very excited when I made a bark for the very first time! I remember this like yesterday and it made all the floors and every wall tremble. It felt like an earthquake. In London they measured 4.2 on the scale of Richter.

When my daddies are at home and neglect me whilst they're playing on their phone or their tablets I have now decided to start barking at them. No no, not once or twice, I mean multiple short, high-pitched, fierce little barks. I keep on barking until they give me lots of cuddles or when they start to play with me. I have proved to them that I can bark for a very long time and I believe they are extremely proud of me. They even give treats to encourage me to bark more and even louder.

I can bark louder than any other dog. I can even bark so loud that my daddies could be given a nuisance order. Obviously I wouldn't push it that far but it's to make you aware how LOUD I can bark.

It's unnecessary to say that when I've met other dogs I have left them completely speechless as a result of my barking.

Sometimes the owners of the dogs were left speechless too and I have seen them cross the road at a very fast pace when I approached them on the lead. I have also witnessed people running to the nearest exit in the park.
One one occasion, when I walked on the seafront, one person jumped into the sea. That person must have been very afraid of me as he was wearing a black rubber-suit, a mask and breathing gear to protect himself.

I have also noticed that birds are frightened of me. Every time when I come near a bird they fly away. Sparrows, black birds, doves, finches and starlings are very afraid of me. The herring seagulls may sometimes prove to be a challenge. It can be very frustrating when they're sitting on the top of my roof but eventually my barking-talent does chase them away.

I have also met a giant tortoise! It lives right across the road. It's name is Onion but doesn't smell like one. Onion has showed me that he can walk pretty fast for a tortoise and I think I'm going to invite him for walkies next time we pass his house.

What a beautiful doggy!

My daddies say that I am a beautiful boy and that I look absolutely gorgeous.

Dear reader, my daddies are speaking the truth. Everybody who has met me kept on saying: "oooh isn't he a beautiful doggie?", "awe isn't he adorable?" or "oh look at him, what a handsome boy!"

People have kindly offered my daddies to look after me whenever they want to go away for a break or a holiday, so that I can live at their home to look after me. It seems that this makes my daddies very happy as it instantly puts a smile on their face but, in the end they always kindly declined their exciting offers.

I wonder why? Nothing is more exciting than to visit someone's else's home where there are no rules. Yeah! I can wee wherever I want to wee! I can chew on carpet, furniture and plants. I can scratch the skirting-boards and the doors. I can sink my teeth into the doormats and I can have a go with the towels. Take me away! Take me with you! Please, please, please! I'm great company!!!

But what if I would get bored? I might miss my home, my favourite food, my people friends and doggie friends. The sea, the White Cliffs and the Downs, the parks, the stones in the garden, my toys and my bed. But most of all … I would miss my gorgeous and loving daddies. The bestest daddies in the world. They are fantastic!

Though, haven't said, if you meet them and you think that I am an adorable, gorgeous and a cute looking boy, just say to my daddies that you would like to look after me and I can promise that you'll be having an amazing time with me!

Socks and towels!

When I was a baby I thoroughly enjoyed attracting my daddies's attention. Every night my daddies would watch DVD's and BluRays whilst they were sitting down on their fat lazy bums ... their lives soon changed from the moment I started living with them.

During my first week at my daddies's house they introduced me to the world of films. They were pointing out their fingers to the TV screen and started saying things like: "Look Buster! Look Buster! Look who is on the TV!" I don't know what got into me but I jumped up against the TV unit and I started barking at whoever appeared on the TV screen. Visitors who came here to play with me from behind the screen come out and play with me! What on earth were they doing in the TV? It's much more exciting to come out and play with me!

I absolutely love to stick my nose into any sock or slipper. The house is very tidy but they both leave one pair of socks out for whoever is going to take me out for a walk the next morning. It's especially great after they've just woken up as my daddies get most upset when I nick one of their socks and usually they start to run after me. Exciting! Exciting! They want to play with me!

Nothing is more exciting than grabbing towels! Towels are heaven. Any towel will do; tea, hand and bath towels. Towels hang normally near sinks, ovens, doors and radiators. When you're really lucky there'll be one on the floor! I normally grab a towel as quick as I can when my daddies are having a chat or when one of them is cooking. Snap! And off I go!
It's great fun to have two men running after you and trying to play with you. It's fun! What I still don't get is why they use towels to dry their hands? I just love to drag it over the floor and play tug with it!

Sometimes I like to play 'hurricane', bouncing off the walls, whirling from one room to another like a small but determined tornado, a fast spinning dynamo and giving my family no peace. Running around like a race-dog from one end to the other end of the house and back again. Yeah! That's great fun! Leaping over the chairs and tables.. Hurray!

I can run, spin around and run until they manage to stop me. I intend to calm down when one of my daddies manages to grab me and indulge me with cuddles. You see, they want me to do it again! Again! And again! I'm spinning around, chasing my tail, move out of my way! This is fantastic!

A trip to
the Animal Doctor
Clarissa

Today was going to be a very exciting day. My daddies would be taking me to the animal doctor in the vroom-vroom! Yesterday I told my friends that I would be visiting the animal doctor. Some of my friends said that they love to visit the doctor but other pals would turn their nose up should they need to visit an animal practice. Some dog-breeds are simply too boring. I would take any opportunity to go out in the vroom-vroom.

I couldn't wait! There was a lovely soft blanket on the back seat of the vroom-vroom and once daddy Michael had attached my collar to the seatbelt we were ready to go. Vroooooooom! The journey took only about ten minutes. I agree that it is far more exciting to walk the same distance in 30 minutes but the vroom-vroom can be very convenient when it rains. Luckily we did go by the vroom-vroom as the rain was coming down in buckets. It didn't stop! I don't like getting wet if there's no need to, unless I go out for my walkies.

We arrived at the animal practise and Daddy Michael parked the car as near to the entrance as he could. He grabbed the massive brolly and opened it whilst he jumped out of the car. He opened the door and removed the seatbelt. I jumped out of the vroom-vroom and was standing underneath the brolly with my daddy. Daddy Richard also jumped out of the vroom-vroom and now all three of us were standing underneath the brolly. It was very nice and dry! We took five steps to the entrance-door and took shelter in the porch. Daddy Michael shook the brolly a couple of times and Daddy Richard opened the entrance door.

I peeked into the doctor's practice and it looked like an amazing big room. I could smell dogs! I could smell cats! Birds! Guinea pigs! Rabbits! Fish! But there was no one to be seen. The room was mine! There were chairs placed against the walls so I had all the space to myself for play. Get my toys. Get my toys! Where are my toys? They didn't leave my toys at home did they?

Daddy Michael opened his bag and 'voila!' there was Lizzy, my favourite toy! Michael threw Lizzy the lizard into the room. I sprinted straight after it and I picked it up with my mouth. I ran back to Daddy Michael and he was trying to get Lizzy out of my mouth. The toy was mine and I would not let it go. We were playing tug and finally Lizzy the lizard slipped from my daddy's hand.

I fell backwards and with ultra-high speed I tumbled over ten times before I ended up against a wall with Lizzy the lizard still in my mouth.

I was laying upside down, head on the floor, paws up against the wall and then suddenly the receptionist's head appeared from behind the desk and her big eyes were looking at me. "Hello lovely boy, are you ok down there? Did you hurt yourself?" Gosh, the lady cares about me. I love this woman! I turned myself around and put the biggest smile on my face. "Yes, I'm fine, thank you". "It's such a relief to hear that you're ok", said the lovely lady, "That was quite a bang wasn't it?" "What's your name?"

"My name is Buster!", I said. "Well you are a real 'buster' aren't you darling. Would you like a little treat?" I sat my bum down on the floor, looked up and her hand was holding a gorgeous smelling turkey treat. I gently took the treat from the receptionist's hand and ran towards my daddies. The receptionist smiled to my daddies and asked them to take a seat. I nestled myself down underneath one of the chairs with my eyes focused on the door which read 'Clarissa the animal doctor'. I was well excited!

It was eleven o'clock. I could hear footsteps behind the door. My tail started waggling and then the door opened. It was her, the animal doctor. "Hello Buster! My name is Clarissa. Welcome to my practice!" My tail was waggling at the fastest speed and I stood up staring at Clarissa. "Come in please". I ran towards the room and started sniffing around. It smelt like Clarissa was hiding an army of cats and dogs in her room but there was no one to be seen. I walked to the door and lifted up my right back leg. "Uh uh uh uh uh!" said Clarissa with a loud voice. I looked up at her with my beautiful dark brown almond shaped eyes whilst I was having a good old wee. I stopped weeing and then ran towards a unit. "You are a naughty boy Buster!" What's the problem? It's perfectly normal for dogs to mark their territory.

The consulting room looked fascinating. There was a weighing scale, a sink, a treat-jar and an examining table. "Come on Buster boy", Clarissa said, "would you like me to put you onto the big table?" I got very excited. She was going to put me onto the big examining table! I reached out my paws and Clarissa lifted me up and put me onto the table. "Let's have a look how healthy you are Buster!" Clarissa touched my ears, looked at my eyes, examined my teeth and she touched my tummy.

I was getting tickles from Clarissa! I like tickles! I love Clarissa! She lifted me up from the examining table and put me onto the weighing scale. "Oh look at your weight Buster, it's perfect! Your fur is lovely and shiny and oh so soft. No fleas, no ticks and no grass. You are very well looked after. You're such a healthy pooch!"
Clarissa looked at my daddies and said: "Buster is perfect! Just carry on feeding him as normal".

"Could I ask what you actually feed him with?" "We feed him dried turkey food, freshly cooked chicken or fish, finely sliced green beans and grated carrot", said Daddy Richard. "That's amazing!, said Clarissa, the combination of dried and fresh food is absolutely fantastic. You are a very lucky doggy Buster! A lot of people don't have the time to prepare fresh food. That's the reason why most people buy dried food and serve it to their pets. A healthy dog, like you, is a happy dog, and a healthy dog has strong, shiny fur". Clarissa then carried on talking about general advice that she gives to all of her clients.

"Your dog's coat is one of the best ways to gain insight into your dog's condition, be it physical or emotional. It's very important to get to know the ideal qualities of your furry friend's breed and to set aside time to maintain his or her coat with regular brushing and giving them a bath only when necessary".

"A balanced diet with plenty of protein and a variety of healthy nutritious ingredients will help strengthen and replenish your dog's coat by giving it a lovely soft and shiny coat. Dog fur is made mostly of protein, so a coat that is dull or fragile can be an indication that your pooch isn't getting the best nutrition. Do your research about the best kind of food and the right portions of it for your dog. If the diet needs an extra boost, you can talk to me about pet supplements".

"Ask yourself am I using the right shampoo for my dog? The fur can be a shelter for ticks, fleas, and other parasites that are very bad for your dog's health. This is especially true in dirty, matted hair. Parasites can lead to infections in your dog. Keep the coat clean and brushed to ensure that parasites stay away".

"The look and feel of the fur aren't the only ways to monitor your dog's health through his coat. The fur should also smell fresh in between baths".

"A strong, musky, or foul odour on dry fur is often an indication of bacterial infection, fungus, fleas, or even dry skin.
A coat that remains stinky even after a scrub is a sign that a visit to me may be in order".

"Keeping your dog's coat strong and shiny will teach you a lot about how to care for his or her health in general. It's a great way to monitor nutrition, win the fight against parasites, and stay informed about your dog's feelings. It's also a wonderful way to bond.
Regular brushing, grooming and petting are all part of their regular needs, so show your dog love and attention for the good of his or her health as well as the good of your relationship with one another".

"I'll give you two anti-worm treatment tablets. You need to give him one tablet every three months. I will also give you six anti-flea treatment capsules that offers combined protection against fleas, lice, mange and ear mites, roundworm and lungworm. Please give him one flea-treatment every month. I'll see you in six months time".

"Please pop in anytime if you want to have him weighed or just to say hello. Some people only take their pet the animal doctor when they need a vaccination. You can imagine that Buster will associate every visit to the practice with an injection and possible stress.
If you pop in every nowadays then Buster will associate most visits with having fun!".

"Now Buster, would you like another treat before you go?" I stood up and showed Clarissa that I can stand on my hind legs. "Oh look at Buster. You're a circus-dog. He is such a good boy!"

I like it here and I'm looking forward to coming back again. We all said goodbye to the animal doctor and when we walked towards the exit the receptionist gave me another treat! I like Clarissa and I like the receptionist. This must be Brighton's most popular vet practice.

Tracie Heart and the Red Speed Demon

I have spent two weeks with my daddies now and ... they love me! They love me! They are there when I wake up and when I go to sleep. They play with me and they feed me. They take me out for walkies and give me tickles and cuddles. They are the best parents in the whole universe!

At 9:00am on the dot they step into the vroom-vroom and it has got two chairs in the front and a large sofa in the back. They use a key which they put into a lock, they turn it which is followed by a loud roar. I love this moment because the sound of the roar reminds me of my daddy Mo-Ja when he used to win a race. After the loud roar my daddies hold a small wheel in their hands and the vroom-vroom with the two chairs and the sofa will start to move forward.

The vroom-vroom uses up a lot of my daddies money. They've taken me out in the vroom-vroom on many occasions and when I was watching through the windows I could see that that vroom-vrooms are virtually everywhere! They are very popular with old people. Baroness Bark had a vroom-vroom too but not as nice as the ones like my daddies have. They've got the best looking vroom-vrooms.

When both my daddies have gone to work I fall asleep on the velvet sofa with the plush cushions. I dream about my daddies and dogs, running through the hills on the South Downs, walking along the cliffs in Saltdean, visiting Chatsworth Park and the pebble beach in Brighton.

Every day at 1:00pm on the dot, a very special somebody comes to visit me. She has a key to the house and when she enters the house there is magic all around her.

This very special somebody is called Tracie Heart. She has the biggest loving heart in the whole wide world. Tracie owns a dog-hotel in Newhaven. The dog-hotel is immensely popular amongst people and dogs in the South-East of England as the rooms are always fully booked. Beside a comfortable sleep-over in one of the most comfortable super-King size beds, Tracie ensures that every dog or cat will get spoilt rotten with the best quality food, the most delicious treats and plenty of cuddles. and kisses. The best part is when she takes all her guests out for walkies during the day. Happy doggies, happy owners.

Tracie also has a very big secret which she hides behind the hotel. It lives in a shed made out of brick and it has two gates which are locked. Tracie is the only person who holds a key to the gates. The thing that lives in the shed made out of brick is a red vroom-vroom and Tracie calls it the Red Speed Demon. Oh yeah! She's got it!

I absolutely love Tracie and the Red Speed Demon. Tracie is my best friend. She adores all pets in the whole universe. Tracie is awesome, she is a woman to my heart. But I still love my daddies's the most.

She has told me that she has a cat who she walks on a lead. She loves her cat very much. She always talks about him when she comes to visit me. I have never ever met the pussycat and I have promised myself that I will never ever meet that cat.
I have decided that I don't like her cat ... at all. Tracie is mine. She has promised that I can live with her forever if I want to. I would love to but only under the condition that the cat has to move out ... permanently.
Tracie always plays with me, cuddles me, feeds me and she is the only person in the world who can tickle me behind my big ears whenever she wants to. These moments can go on forever and ever.

Every time after we have greeted each other the moment arrives when Tracie's puts on my collar, opens the front door and then ... we run down the stairs towards the Red Speed Demon! The engine is already running, the roof is pulling backwards and the doors open automatically to take me and Tracie for a ride! The red vroom-broom has two chairs which are very soft and comfortable. These chairs are almost like upholstered leather sofas in which you can relax. I'm in doggy-heaven every time when I sit down on my seat. Tracie has put a cashmere cushion on it to keep me warm.
The doors close automatically once Tracie has taken her seat behind the plate. The engine starts to roar and the demon starts to move forward very fast. Before you realise it moves faster than the speed of the light! The demon can talk too and it tells us to fasten our seat belts. I'm always excited but this is the moment where I get really excited!!! Let the countdown begin: five, four, three, two and one and yo yo yo here we go! Straight into the air!

Hurray! Yippee! We're off for a ride through the skies of the South of England!

My neighbour Reginald was tidying up his front garden. He looked around him after he heard a noise that sounded like an aeroplane which just took off. Reg was not aware of any nearby airports. He looked up and then he spotted the Red Speed Demon. That's what it was! It was a lovely day and the roof was down. Reg spotted me and waved his hand at us. Other neighbours opened their front doors and walked into their gardens. They were all waiving at us. Neighbour Jo said that she was baking doggy biscuits in the oven for when I would get back. Neighbour Trevor said he would clear our pathway so it would all look nice and neat again upon my return. Neighbour David said he would be washing the windows and neighbour Fiona promised to give the porch way a good swipe with her broom stick.

My neighbours were the bestest neighbours anyone could have. They're superstars!

We were off. Tracie stopped at two other houses to collect my pals Sean the Basset Hound and Bessie the Golden Retriever. This was going to be an exciting time!

We flew over the Brighton Pier where I could see people having fun in the helter-skelter, eating ice cream and soaking up the sunshine on the beach-chairs. We zig-zagged our way through the Marine Drive arches and waved to the people on the Volks Railway train at Brighton Marina. We followed our way along the White cliffs and the Red Speed Demon landed in Saltdean. We all jumped out of the car and ran towards the sea where we played on the pebbled beach. This was a fun day! Tracie said that she had the rest of the day off so she decided that we should visit Eastbourne. We flew over Newhaven, Seaford, Alfriston and yeah, right over the steep hill I could see Eastbourne.

Tracie kept it as surprise that the World Tour Women's tennis tournament was taking place today at the Devonshire Park Lawn Tennis Club, Eastbourne. I spotted Belinda and Agnieszka playing tennis on the outdoor grass courts. It looked like they were doing a 'warm-up" for the Wimbledon Grand Slam event!

The Red Speed Demon flew over the tennis-grounds and Belinda threw a tennis ball up in the air. That ball looked exactly like my tennis ball.

I jumped up from my seat and was standing on my hind legs. The ball reached it's top and started to come down. I was jumping up and down like a kangaroo and then suddenly the ball came towards me and - SNAP - I caught the tennis ball between my teeth!

I looked down and Belinda was clapping her hands. "Good boy!'Good boy!', she was saying with a big smile on her face. Agnieszka threw her ball up in the air too which was caught by Sean. I love tennis balls! From now on this one is my favourite tennis ball! I love Belinda!

They waived goodbye to us and the Red Speed Demon took us for a ride to the Seven Sisters and the White Cliffs of Dover. 140 miles per hour and listening to the Foo Fighters. Perfect! The sun was shining and the white cliffs looked bright and shiny. I had to wear my sunglasses to protect my eyes from the dazzling sun light. I could see the sheep hopping around in the fields, the rabbits were chasing each other and I could see ramblers climbing the hills in the Downs. The Red Speed Demon suddenly made a U-turn. Tracie's time was up and the vroom-vroom brought us back home. We landed right in front of my house and I ran back to the front door. Tracie followed swiftly and opened the front door. Tracie gave me lots of cuddles and said: "We did have a ball didn't we Buster?" I sat myself down on the floor. My tail was waggling. Tracie opened her handbag and put her hand into it. My tail was now waggling faster. I could smell turkey! Tracie took her hand out of the bag and she held a very tasty treat in front of me. My tail was waggling at the fastest speed by now and before she could say a word I went into a down-position. "Oh you"re such a good and clever boy! This treat is especially for you!" I gently grabbed the delightful turkey treat between my teeth and started chewing it. This was yummy. Tracie gave me lots of cuddles and kisses and said: "You are such a sweetheart. I'll be back tomorrow. Be a good boy!" Tracie walked back to the Red Speed Demon. She stepped into the vroom-vroom and waived goodbye to me. The doors closed automatically once Tracie had taken her seat behind the wheel.

The engine started to roar and the demon started to move forward very fast. Even faster than the speed of the light!

Guru George

Head Master

I was six months old when my daddies decided that it was time for me to take part in agility and obedience classes. Until today I still don't understand why they thought I needed to attend classes. I remember it was December and my daddies took me out for Christmas shopping. The shops were absolutely jam-packed with people looking for the most wonderful and precious gifts. People were talking, laughing and singing along to the Christmas carols which you could hear through the speakers in the shops. The atmosphere was fabulous.

I honestly didn't have any reason to grab the attention of hundreds of shoppers after I started howling and screaming (without stopping) after I spotted another dog in the shop. I just wanted to play and be friends with the gorgeous looking white poodle. I had no intention to embarrass my daddies and neither did I want them to leave the garden centre instantly without any Christmas gifts. I just wanted to have fun!

It was in February on the coldest day of the year when they decided to take me to the agility and obedience classes run by a gentleman called Guru George. It was very dark outside and the wind was blowing. They took me out for an exciting ride in the vroom-vroom in the evening. When my daddies stopped the vroom-vroom they took me out of it, put on the lead and there I was standing in front of a temple covered in ice. Brrrrrrrrr!
We walked slowly towards the dark wooden gates of the temple. The wind was howling around the exotic looking structure. The temple had four pavilions on each corner and it had huge windows on each side which reached from the floor to ceiling. The golden curtains prevented me from seeing what was going inside.

I was only a few steps from the entrance when I suddenly could hear a loud sound. I barked and could feel the vibration from the sound in the ground underneath me. The sound came from behind the dark wooden gates. I stood behind my daddies watching what was going on and there was the same sound again. The sound was nearer now. It was followed by another loud sound, and another one and another one. Every time when I heard the sound it was getting louder and it was coming closer to the wooden gates. There were two more sounds and then all of a sudden it stopped.
There was something standing right behind the wooden gates now.

By this time I had become ecstatic and I was holding my breath. I couldn't hold my breath too long so I gasped for more air and I was holding my breath again in utter excitement for what was going to happen next.

Suddenly the doors started to open and a beam of light illuminated the outside area.

The air filled itself with thin smoke that smelt of roses. The smoke got thicker and the wind was playing with it. The outside area was turned into a mysterious foggy scene. The gates were now wide open and a silhouette started to move forward. Then, emerging from the smoke at the entrance, a giant arose. He looked like a massive 30 feet high statue of a Dvarapala. The giant was standing in the door opening with his arms crossed over his chest. Between his eye brows and bushy moustache I could see his eyes which were staring at me with a look like 'I could eat you raw'!

The Dvarapala* (see page 49) started to talk and with a deep loud voice he said: "My name is Guru George and I am the Head Master of the School for Doggies. I am your leader and counsellor and I'll help you to mould values and behaviour. I'll help you to discover the best within you. I'll be your guide and will help you on your way to become a well behaved doggy. Your Head Master Guru George has spoken".

Oh my gosh, that voice of Guru George made the ground tremble underneath me.

It had left me completely flabbergasted! The tulips and daffodils in the grass looked a little bit shaken as well.

Would it be polite to give an answer to Guru George? But what would I say? Errrm, thank you for becoming my master? Guru George my master? Head Master of the School of Doggies? Buster is the Master. Not Mr George. I'm also very well behaved. Why am I here? Are we having a laugh? Hahahaha. Hahahaha. I can't stop laughing!

The classes run by Guru George were a true challenge and he required me to be there at 7:00pm on the dot. Every Monday and Tuesday evening I had to give up my beauty sleep in order to attend the School for Doggies.

I am hooked on sleeping after a tough day of playing, eating and walkies. That was normally my-time. Buster-time.

Spending time with Guru George was very daunting at first, but during the first class I met a lot of new doggies. There were small and large dogs. Beagles and Spaniels, Huskies and Labradors. I got all excited during the evening and I can reveal that I could not stop barking! Barking is one of my favourite things. I love to bark! I didn't stop that evening! Guru George was very interested in me and he had a long one to one with my daddy Michael during that evening. I'm special! I'm so special!

However, later that evening, when we got home, Daddy Michael told Daddy Richard that he wasn't too sure whether he would be going back to Master Guru George's classes. I was completely puzzled. I got Guru George's attention, all evening. I'm a beautiful boy, I'm sweet and I'm gorgeous. Guru George told Daddy Michael that he would run a special class, just for me and Daddy Michael. He could do this on a Saturday. I started to take a shine to Guru George. This man was something special! One-to-one classes on Saturdays.
Oh yes I woof! I later discovered that barking all the time during class was not pleasing to my Daddy Michael or the other people which is why I had special classes.

After three classes I totally worshipped Guru George. He was magnificent. I would do everything for Guru George, even stop barking all the time, which is one of my favourite things.

Guru George also introduced me to ... cheese! Creamy, delicious, fat cheese. It was much easier to consume compared to the dry and virtually fat-free treats my daddies gave me as a reward for sits, ups and downs. Cheese was the word. Cheese it is. I would do anything for cheese. I would do anything for Guru George.

So I did! I learned to obey to sit down properly with my bum down on the floor. I learned how to lay down and I learned to wait before I was fed my food and I learned to wait before crossing the roads. I love Guru George! I'm a good boy! Just give me more and more cheese!

After working the basic dog obedience course I was awarded the puppy foundation award, the bronze & silver award and now on my way to gold. It was a fantastic way of spending as much time as I could with Daddy Michael, Guru George and all my friends and their owners! I really enjoyed it. Dog training clubs are usually very sociable, where groups of like-minded people and their dogs meet on a regular basis, and get great enjoyment in training. Most of these clubs will welcome all standards of handlers and dogs to be trained. Guru George welcomed any kind of dog, even the dogs that had driven other dog trainers completely mad! Guru George loves all the dogs in the world.
He told me that I was his most favourite dog!

* Dvarapala (Sanskrit) is a door or gate guardian often portrayed as warrior or fearsome asura giant, usually armed with a weapon like a long sword. The statue of dvarapala is a widespread architectural element throughout the Hindu and Buddhist cultures, as well as in the areas influenced by them like Java.

An afternoon tea with the Queen

Today is the day of all days: it's my 1st birthday! It's party-time! My biggest wish was to celebrate this great event in the Queen's palace and therefore I asked my daddies to write a letter to Her Royal Highness to find out whether I could use the palace whilst the Queen and her family would be away on holiday. I thought it would be an amazing idea if I could look after the Queen's house and her beautiful corgis.

The letter was sent by special delivery and required a signature. Oh wouldn't it be exciting if the Queen would sign for the letter herself. Fingers crossed that she will be delighted with my suggestion and simply says 'yes'!

Three days later at 10:00am in the morning I could hear footsteps in the front garden. I recognised those steps. They were from the postman. Every morning he delivers our mail.

My Daddy Richard was at home and I sprinted to the front door to make him aware that the postman just had delivered the post. I was well excited! Daddy Richard walked into the hallway. He grabbed his keys from the hallway table and opened the front door. Did the postman deliver a letter for me today? I would soon find out. I couldn't wait!!!
Daddy Richard opened the letterbox in the porch and took the post out. A big silk envelope, with a gold engraved crown on it, fell down on the floor. I spotted that my name was on it! This could be the letter I was waiting for. Daddy Richard kneeled down and picked up the letter. I didn't let the letter out of my sight. Daddy Richard held the letter in front of me and said: "This letter is for Buster! Come on and take it into the dining room!" I grabbed it and ran back into the hallway taking the second turn left into the dining room. I put the letter on the floor and laid down in front of it.

I could read that the letter was addressed to Master Buster and it had a stamp on it with a picture of the Royal palace! This must be the letter I have been waiting for. It was time to ... open it! Normally I rip my teeth through any letters in a second but this time I had to open the envelope carefully to ensure that I wouldn't damage the letter so I could read every word of it. I gently opened the edges of the envelope with my teeth and with my front paws I managed to lift the letter out which opened with the words:

"My dearest Buster,

It's the first time in my entire reign of this country that I have received correspondence from a dog and I am pleased to inform you that I am utterly delighted.

I, the monarch, am very grateful to you for making the suggestion to look after my palace during my stay abroad with my family. You are a very special dog and I would like to ensure that my corgis, who are my family too, would have been delighted with the idea.

Due to unforeseen circumstances I regret to announce that I have postponed my holiday. Therefore the services you've kindly offered would be no longer required.

I can understand that you may be very disappointed that you are not able to organise your very first birthday party in my palace. However, I am delighted to write that you are allowed to celebrate your birthday in my private garden.

You, your parents and your friends regardless of whether they are human or canine are invited to Her Royal Majesty's garden party. You'll be provided with a beautiful selection of mouthwatering finger sandwiches and delicious sweet treats including carrot cakes and a selection of freshly baked scones from the Royal Scone recipe of buttermilk, lavender, and parmesan and wholemeal orange and honey. An Afternoon Tea simply to die for.

Please acknowledge in writing or respond to me via social media.

I would be delighted meeting you and your friends.

Yours sincerely,

The Queen."

Yeah! I'm invited to celebrate my 1st birthday party at the Queen's gardens.
Daddy Richard, please read this letter! Daddy Richard picked up the letter, read it thoroughly and jumped up in the air. "Eureka!", he shouted excitedly. Daddy picked me up and threw me up in the air three times shouting "Hurray! Hurray! Hurray!" He gave me lots of cuddles and a treat!

He picked up his mobile phone and texted Daddy Michael about the invitation from the Queen. Daddy Michael who was always very busy at work texted back within one minute and said that he was jubilant!

The Queen has two birthdays, her actual birthday and an official one. I have two birthdays too! My actual birthday is in July and the official one is in September when I came to live with my two new daddies. On both days I get lots of gifts. Maybe I'm of royal blood too, like the Queen. Everyone says I look like a prince and my daddies even got married in a palace, so maybe it's true.

I have sent all my doggy-friends and their parents in the neighbourhood an invitation for an amazing day full of fun. I can't wait!

The day has arrived. Today is my birthday. My daddies woke up extra early at six o'clock this morning and they had decorated the house with balloons, banners, bunting and noisemakers. They've even created goody-bags and ... there were plenty of poo-bags too! All my friends in the neighbourhood arrived around ten o'clock and we were all barking, sniffing each other and playing with each other.

At eleven o'clock we could hear a big vroom-vroom arriving. It was Tracie Heart!
She stepped out of the big red vroom-vroom and gave me lots of cuddles and kisses.
I love Tracie Heart! She then cuddled every other dog and said hello to all our guests.
My daddies made her a cup of Early Grey tea and served it with a home-made biscuit.
Tracie enjoyed the tea and the biscuit very much and after she finished her cuppa she said that it was time to head off to a journey to the Queen in the Red Speed Demon!

I felt so privileged to have been invited to one of Her Royal Majesty's garden parties. I can imagine a beautiful selection of mouthwatering finger sandwiches and delicious sweet treats including carrot cakes and a selection of freshly baked scones from the Royal Scone recipe.

I was seated on my cashmere cushion and everybody else was settled on the seats of the Red Speed Demon. The doors closed automatically once Tracie had taken her seat behind the wheel. Before we realised it moved faster than the speed of the light! The engine started to roar and the demon started to move forward very fast.

Let the countdown begin: five, four, three, two and one and yo yo yo up we go straight into the air! Hurray! Yippee! We're off to the Queen's garden party!

We were only five minutes up in the air when we could hear a stuttering sound coming from the vroom-vroom. Daddy Michael & Daddy Richard looked at Tracie. Tracie looked at my daddies and then she looked at the dashboard.
"Oh dear me", Tracie said.
"What's up?" asked Daddy Richard.
"I forgot that the Red Speed Demon didn't close his eyes last night. I was house-sitting for the two Irish setters in Saltdean and I took them out for a night-ride. The Red Speed Demon needs a rest! The dashboard is indicating that he needs a good old nap!"
"Oh poor Red Speed Demon", said Daddy Michael. "Would a power-nap be ok? Perhaps five or ten minutes and then we can continue our journey to the Queen. "
"I'm really sorry, said Tracie, but the dash-board indicates that the Red Speed Demon needs to recharge his batteries for at least four hours. I'm so so sorry!"

Everybody looked a little bit disappointed. It was just ten minutes after 11:00 am and we were still flying through the air-space of Brighton.

"Look! Look over there!", said Tracie pointing her finger down to Stanmer Park.

"Look it's Jeremy and David!" I looked down from the window and yes I could see them too!

Not only could I see Jeremy and David, I could also see dozens of Miniature Schnauzers!!!

"Hi Tracie!", said Jeremy. "Would you like to come and join us for a Schnauzer-Fest Tea Party in Stanmer House?"

"Oh yes we would love too!" Tracie put the vroom-vroom in it's lowest gear and landed right in front of the house where Jeremy, David and thirty six miniature schnauzers greeted me with a lot of barks, sniffs and play.

My favourite pal Otto, the white Miniature Schnauzer and his parents Kate & Steve were there too! We greeted each other and ran through the trees into the fields. We ran and we ran and then we ran back to the group. Daddy Michael & Richard were talking to Jeremy and David and Otto and I greeted their Miniature Schnauzers Trevor and Geof.

Then we met Deborah and her beautiful little princess miniature Schnauzer Daisy Belle. We've met each other before and I think I've got a bit of a crush on Daisy Belle!

We said hello and did a lot of sniffing. Then Otto spotted Izzy! They were all here today.

Izzy is my other favourite friend and she joined the party with her mothers Ceri & Jenna.

All afternoon we were playing with each other in the woods and eating chews, doggy biscuits and treats whilst my daddies and the other daddies and mummies were having a proper Sunday Roast. This was so much fun! What an amazing way to celebrate my birthday!

At 4:00 pm Tracie came over to me to tell me that the Red Speed Demon had just woken up and wanted to take us for a ride through the sky! Everybody got well excited and they all started to take their seats in the vroom-vroom.

Suddenly I could hear galloping noises coming from the air. I looked up and saw a golden carriage being pulled by four magical white horses. From the window a hand with a white glove was waiving at me.

When the carriage came closer and descended itself onto the park grounds I finally saw that it was the Queen!

I jumped out of the Red Speed Demon, walked over to the golden carriage and kneeled down in front of the Queen. The Queen looked at me from the window and said:
"My dearest Buster. I was very sorry to hear that you were unable to attend the Royal Tea Garden party because the Red Speed Demon was in need of a good old nap.
Therefore I decided to visit you in person to send you my warmest birthday wishes.
I hope you and all your friends had a wonderful time in Stanmer Park.
I'll be in touch with you to re-arrange a date so we can all meet up some time soon".
Buster was very taken by the Queen's words and said: "I'm very grateful to Her Royal Highness. You have been very generous to me".
"It was a pleasure", she said and then the Queen opened the door of the carriage.
She stretched out her arms and said: "Please come over here and give Ma'am a good cuddle before I return to the palace!" We cuddled and cuddled and the Queen's clothes smelt of roses. Oops, perhaps I should not have mentioned this. I kissed the Queen's hand before she closed the door of her golden carriage and she sett off with her white magical horses to bring her back to the palace.
"Cheerio Master Buster!" the Queen said.
"Goodbye Your Royal Majesty!", I said and I waived my little paws as fast as I could.
I waived and waived until the carriage disappeared on the horizon.

"Come on, hurry up Buster, off we go!", said Tracie. Daddy Michael & Richard were standing next to the Red Speed Demon and we were pointing at the cashmere cushion on the back seat. I jumped onto the cushion and my daddies jumped onto the backseat next to me. Everybody was in the car, Otto, Izzy, Daisy Belle, Trevor & Geof and everyone else.

The doors closed automatically once Tracie had taken her seat behind the wheel.
The engine started to roar and the demon started to move forward very fast. Before we realised it moved faster than the speed of the light!
Let the countdown begin: five, four, three, two and one and yo yo yo up we go!
Straight into the air! Hurray! Yippee! Let's go for a ride!

Surprise-Saturday and the secret of the Goldstone

Today my daddies told me that we were going to do something very special next week Saturday. Yay! We were going to do something special in only one week's time!
I was already in the highest state of excitement although I didn't have a single clue about what was going to happen.
Everyday I woke up and I was counting down the days until it was Surprise-Saturday.
I always wake up at 6:55am on the dot, because I know that five minutes later one of my daddies would jump out of bed, get themselves dressed, put their socks and shoes on and then, they'll take me out for ... walkies!

Today was the Saturday of all Saturdays. Something really exciting was going to happen!
I decided to wake up at 5:00am as I was filled with excitement about that something special that was going to happen. I started to bounce around like a kangaroo and bark which not only caused my daddies to wake up, but even the neighbours Reg, Jo, Trevor, David and Fiona. I couldn't help it but I honestly never had the intention to wake up my daddies and the lovely neighbours who all had left their beds to come over to our front garden to find out what on earth was going on.

Daddy Richard switched the bedside lamp on and the room filled with a soft gentle light. The concerned neighbours were standing outside in front of the semi-lit bedroom window. They could see a shadow behind the curtains which was continuously bouncing up and down. Peeking between a gap in the curtains next door neighbour David looked at Trevor, Jo looked at Fiona and Reg and they all burst out laughing. The neighbours suddenly realised it was me who was bouncing up and down in the bedroom and making all the noises. They were all giggling and said to each other that they would be going back home. They kindly whispered to me to go back to sleep as it was very early in the morning and Saturdays are meant for people to have a lay-in.

I pretended to go back to sleep and was still bouncing around in my mind. Eventually it was 6:55am. I stood up and I jumped off the bed. I ran towards the front door and put my paws up against the door. Slowly and softly I scratched my paws down on the front door which made a fantastic screeching noise like nails scratching down a blackboard. I'm so excited.

After Daddy Richard had taken me out for a walk, so I could have a good sniff around in the neighbourhood and check everything was OK, they served me with …. breakfast! I get fed twice a day, at 7:30am and 6:00pm. By 7:30am I've been without food for 13 hours! However, I do get treats in between the meals when I do a trick or behave really well for my daddies.

My food is made by Daddy Richard from freshly cooked Waitrose chicken breast or coley fish, the finest green beans (manually sliced) and grated Chantilly carrots. They also give me the bestest dried dog-food that is made out of turkey, linseeds, beetroot, rice and so many other nutritious ingredients. By the time you've started reading this page I will have finished my breakfast. I eat extremely fast, like any other dog. If another dog would come into the kitchen they would attempt to eat MY food so it's best to get any food into me as soon as I can. I would not recommend this to the humans as they have learned to be patient. You probably understand that the real reason why I ate so fast is because I've not had had any food over the last 13 hours! Except treats of course but that doesn't count!

It is Surprise-Saturday today and I can't wait to find out what is going to happen! It must be very exciting because my daddies told me last week that we were going to do something very special today. Yay!

The daddies were going into the front garden of the house to get the orange vroom-vroom ready. They put the fluffiest Egyptian towels onto the backseat and to top it all up, they put down the softest cashmere cushions. I knew by now that we were going out somewhere nice with the vroom-vroom! This was going to be well exciting!

Daddy Richard said with a very exciting voice: "Buster, we're going to do something amazing today. Today we'll be visiting … Hove Park!" OMG! We were going to Hove Park!

The first time when my daddies took me to this park I met their friend Angie E.D. and her dog Bruno. Angie was lovely, smiley and chatty. She would always wear the latest designer clothes accompanied by dazzling jewellery. Bruno wore a beautiful shiny diamond collar and we became best of friends!

61

We had lots of play on the grounds of the park. At the end of the afternoon we went to the miniature steam railway for a ride on the miniature steam train! We waved to all the visitors and their dogs in the park and the biggest surprise was that we went through a real tunnel! I couldn't wait to go back to Hove Park for a day packed with fun!

The park has become immensely popular with local residents, dogs and runners. It features a mix of large areas of open grass, mature trees, flower beds and recreational facilities. It's a fantastic place as I can play around with other dogs and run around through the open grass. I enjoyed it so much that my daddies said that we were going to visit Hove Park for the second time and I was so looking forward to it!

Daddy Michael parked the vroom-vroom at the entrance of the park and I jumped from the backseat onto the grass. I sprinted to the nearest tree for a wee. I heard a bark, a very familiar bark and then I saw my pal Otto coming from behind the trees. Yay! Otto the white miniature schnauzer was here! We nosed each other and said "Let's go and play in the fields!" Off we went, bouncing around like two kangaroos.
Then Otto's mum and dad Kate and Steve came running towards me and gave me a lot of cuddles and a big hug. Otto and I started to play in the grass whilst my daddies said hello to Kate and Steve. We were all so excited to be here.
I have to tell you that Hove Park is an amazing park but it is also full of mysterious bushy areas, shrubs and I suspect rabbit and fox holes underneath the ground.

When Otto and I were sniffing our way through the leaves on the ground we literally bumped into a massive piece of stone. Eeek! There was a rock, right here in the park. It looked like a meteor had landed in Hove Park. If it was a meteor I wondered how long it had taken for the falling star to reach the park.

The rock was a very large stone. Otto and I walked around the rock and I could see that it was covered in golden dust. It was set on its side in the centre of a ring of nine smaller stones. Could this have been used as an ancient pick-nick table by Giants? It all looked very mysterious to me. Otto and I had become very curious about the story behind this massive piece of stone.

I looked up to the stone and suddenly I could see a sign which was placed in front of the rock. There was something written on the sign. It read:

GOLDSTONE

TOLMEN

OR THE

HOLY STONE OF DRUIDS

This sounded pretty interesting to me. I think we've just discovered a new Stonehenge in Brighton & Hove! Otto and I looked at each other and we started chasing each other around the big stone and looping around the nine smaller stones. My daddies told me that this would be an exciting day!

Suddenly a crow flew over and settled itself down on one of the branches of the tree near the rock formation. "I guess you didn't expect to find that big stone to be here right in front you?" said the crow. I told Mr Crow that it was amazing to discover such a massive object in the middle of the. Park.

"Let me tell you a little bit more about the history of this rock.", said the crow.

I couldn't wait to find out more about this mysterious stone and was very eager to find out what Mr Crow had to tell us.

"Well", said the crow, "according to the myths, one day the Devil was digging his way into Devil's Dyke, which you know is the big hill north of Brighton & Hove. He wanted to let in the sea through the Downs to flood the churches and drown the people in the villages. He stubbed his toe on the gold rock and in anger kicked it over the hills. The rock landed in an area what is now known as Goldstone Valley".

I looked shocked and the crow could tell from the expression on my face that I was very worried about what may have happened in the past.

The crow continued: "Don't worry Buster, it's only a myth, one of many".

"There is another myth which states that the stone was used as a place of worship for druids. In the 19th century people believed this 'Goldstone' was thought to be a sacred stone of the druids. The news spread fast and the story attracted large numbers of people visiting Devil's Dyke and unfortunately they caused a lot of damage to the surrounding farm crops. In early 1800 the farmer and landowner Mr Rigden was so fed up with everything that he decided to burry the stone and the smaller surrounding stones to put an end to the nosy people who were damaging his farm crops".

"The stones lay secretly buried from the people for nearly a hundred years. Most of the people in East-Sussex had totally forgotten about the existence of the Druid stones though, the story was still being told during history classes at the local schools around Devils Dyke. The children told their parents about the gold stones but many considered the story to be a fairytale as the stones were never ever seen by a living soul".
"It wasn't until early 1900 when a nine year old girl told her father archeologist Mr Dick Digger about the stones. Mr Digger believed the words of his daughter and went to the old monastery in Devils Dyke and spent day after day looking through the old parchment history paperwork to find out what may have happened to the special stones. On the seventh day he discovered that the gold stone formation was buried on the land of Mr Rigden, the former landowner. Archeologist Digger found out about their position. He hired a team of archaeologists and dug up all the land of the former farmer and landowner. The stones were found the following day.
In 1906 the stones were put on display here where you are now in Hove Park".
That's how Mr Crow finished this fascinating story.

Otto and I put our paws up and gave a big applause to Mr Crow for revealing the myths behind the mysterious rock. The Goldstone stones have found a permanent place in Hove Park where everybody can admire them.
"What an amazing story Mr Crow! Thank you so much for sharing this great story with me and my friend Otto!" "It was a pleasure Mr Buster", said Mr Crow.

Daddy Richard came running towards the stones, followed by Michael, Kate and Steve. "They are here, near the rock formation. I found Buster and Otto", said Richard. "Yay! We finally found them!", said Kate. Buster was very excited to see his daddies again and Otto was over the moon to see his mum and dad. Everybody was so happy!
"Let's go to Hangleton Manor and have lunch!", said Michael, "Buster and Otto are allowed in too". "Oh yes that would be fabulous!", said Kate and Steve, "We can't wait!"

Mr Crow made a loud screech in the hope to grab Buster's attention. Buster looked up to the branch where Mr Crow was still sitting. "Mr Buster. Let me tell you another little story, this story is about the Manor House where you are going to have your lunch. It's one of the oldest buildings in Hove dating back to the 15th century. The local folklore tells that a 17th-century dovecote in the grounds has been haunted ever since a monk placed a curse on it. Are you absolutely sure you want to go there, Mr Buster?" I looked very scared and the story from Mr Crow left me a little bit shaken. Oh dear Me. Hangleton Manor had been cursed! Otto looked a little afraid too.

Mr Crow continued his story: "The story goes that the monk was angered by the poos which were left by the birds and so he placed a curse on it. Since then, the building has been haunted by ghost pigeons".
I raised my eyebrows up and straightened my ears. Did I hear the word pigeons? I'm sure I did. Pigeons! The dovecote is being visited by pigeons. I'm not afraid of pigeons. I love chasing pigeons! Yeah, let's go to the Manor House where all the dogs are welcome.

Richard, Michael, Kate, Steve, Otto and me went for a walk to Hangleton Manor and as it happened, many other people and their dogs joined us during the walk. When we arrived we all settled down in Hangleton Manor and we all had a fabulous lunch.
Otto and I were served a mini-roast with the most delicious turkey breast, glazed carrots, steamed green beans and crispy potatoes baked in goose fat! We didn't see any ghost pigeons but we did see a few real ones after lunch!

Hurray! Hurray!
It's a Summer Holiday!

The bees and the birds are out, the sun is shining, it's warm and everybody was friendly and lovely. It's Summer! A fresh wind blows into the house through the open windows and the green string door-curtain is swaying in the breeze, it looks like it's dancing in the wind like a palm-tree. When daddy Michael is home he takes me into the garden and I can put my paws up and simply doze off.

My daddies have booked a Summer-Holiday and they've promised me that they'll announce soon where we would be going to. I can not wait!!! They've told me about their previous holidays in Amsterdam, Aruba, San Francisco, Marrakesh, Florida-Orlando, Paris, Barcelona and Mykonos.
I so want to know where we would be going to!

Well, I found out the same day. Let me tell you that this will become another great adventure! We were going to a big holiday house in Holland!* This was well exciting!!!
Both my daddies have been to Holland before because part of their family lives there. My Daddy Richard is Dutch and he always speaks that strange language when he talks to Dadda and Mumma Buijs in Holland. Their language sound almost exactly like the language they speak in the TV series The Bridge. It sounds like anything but English! Daddy Michael can only say a few phrases in Dutch but understands more than he lets on.

* The name Holland is used to refer to the country The Netherlands. They are the same country. In the past Holland was a county which was ruled by the Counts of Holland.
By the 17th century, Holland had risen to become a maritime and economic power.
The area of the former County of Holland was stretched over the two Dutch provinces of North-Holland and South-Holland, which together include the country's largest cities: Amsterdam, Rotterdam, The Hague and Utrecht. It doesn't matter whether Amsterdam is in Holland or The Netherlands, it's the same country after all .

Dutch is one of the closest relatives of both the German and the English languages. I'm a dog and I only speak doggy-language but I understand most other languages. We dogs always understand each other whatever we're saying whether we are in the UK or in Spain. Dutch is widely spoken in Holland, Belgium, Suriname, and in the Caribbean islands (Aruba, Curaçao and Sint Maarten).

Now, I told you that we're going to Holland!!! To me this land is famous because of its most delicious cheeses in the world like Edam, Gouda and Leerdammer. Yummy! I'm hooked on cheese. Fat, creamy, soft, scrumptious and deliciously tasting cheese. I'm going to love this country! My daddies sat down with me on the big sofa and we had a look through the photos of the house we would be staying in called the Holland House. It is a big house made out of brick walls and it has a very high gable roof with dormers all made of wood. The house stands next to a massive lake and a large orchard full of apple trees.

There is lots of grass around the house so I could play and there are hundreds of trees which I could use for hundreds of weewees. Daddy Richard has been in contact with the owner of the house Lady Annie Key and she was looking forward seeing us over the Summer-Holiday in the Holland House.

The day of all days had arrived. We were going on a Summer-Holiday to Holland!!! My daddies packed up the boot of the vroom-vroom with my basket, my sheep cloth, my giraffe cushion, my toys Big Ted, Lizzy the lizard, Teddy, Red rope, mini rope, bottle, Rudolph, my antler, my food and my water and food bowls. There was just enough space left for my daddies's suitcases. I was seated on the sofa on my cashmere cushions and my daddies were sitting on their front-seats. We were ready to go for our trip to Holland.

The journey in the vroom-vroom was amazing! The sun was shining and the air-conditioning was on. We were listening to music from Kylie Minogue, Pet Shop Boys, Robbie Williams, Little Mix, David Bowie and Ellie Goulding. We travelled through Eastbourne, Hastings and Ashford, making plenty of stops, before we arrived at the White Cliffs of Dover.

There were a lot of other people and dogs on the top of the White Cliffs of Dover.
I played with other dogs and I did lots of running exercises before we would be crossing the
English Channel. After my play-session I said goodbye to all the doggies and we all went
back to the vroom-vroom to continue our journey. Daddy Michael drove us near to the edge
of the white cliffs and parked behind a lot of other vroom-vrooms. Wooden fences were
placed about ten feet from the edge of the cliffs to make sure that the vroom-vrooms would
not accidentally fall off the cliffs. The sun was still beaming its glorious heat down and we
were waiting in the vroom-vroom full of excitement to carry on with our journey to Holland.

The Border Controller walked along by the vroom-vrooms and was handing over tickets to
everybody. When the Border Controller walked towards us, the vroom-vroom opened its
window automatically.
The Border Controller asked: "Where are you travelling to today?" Daddy Michael
responded: "We're going to Holland! The country where the windmills keep on turning and
where people give each other tulips from Amsterdam!"
"I wish I could come along with you. I have heard some many great stories about Holland.
Please send my bestest regards to the King and Queen should you see them."
"Of course we will", said Daddy Richard. The Border Controller handed over our tickets.

"Yay!", shouted Daddy Richard, "look Michael we got the tickets for the Channel Road
Bridge!"
Daddy Richard sounded so happy that, whatever Channel Road Bridge meant, this promised
to be something really exciting! By now everybody had received their tickets and
the Border Controller opened the gates. The vroom-vrooms couldn't wait any longer to
enter the road which was going down alongside the cliffs towards the seafront.

It only took two minutes to get down to the beach and I must say that the views were stunning. Behind me were the White Cliffs of Dover and in front of me was the biggest swimming pool I had ever seen!

The road was created in a way that we automatically ended up in the queue to enter the Channel Road Bridge. People drove their vroom-vroom on something that looked like a rotating staircase which took them right up to the entrance of the bridge. Electric grippers picked up the vroom-vrooms from the top of the staircase and placed them onto the Channel Road Bridge. Every time when the conductor blew his whistle a vroom-vroom would drive off.

Over one million happy dogs and cats have already travelled over the Channel Road Bridge and finally I was going to cross the massive swimming pool called the English Channel. Our vroom-vroom was picked up by the electric grippers and was placed on the Channel Road Bridge. The whistle blew and off we went!

The journey went well fast. There were white herring seagulls flying high up in the sky and I saw dolphins and seals swimming next to the bridge. Before I realised it we reached land. We arrived in a new country which was called 'La France'.

'La France', according to the posters, is all about fashion, men and ladies with dogs, alfresco dining, wine, perfume and romance. La vie en rose.

Our first destination in France was Calais. The town Calais overlooks the Strait of Dover and is the closest French town to England. It was a bright day and I could easily see the White Cliffs of Dover from Calais. We went to brasserie Café de Paris to sit down for a cup of French coffee and a bowl of fresh water. The waiter gave me a treat, a sweet and creamy thing, called a macaroon. That was yummy. That was delicious! I love macaroons! I hope my daddies would stock up the vroom-vroom up with plenty of those macaroons.

I had a look through the pictures of the French magazines at the brasserie and I came to the conclusion that some things were slightly different in France compared to the United Kingdom. The UK is a country where people have a cup of tea and porridge for breakfast but in France people have a bottle of wine, drink hot chocolate from a soup bowl and eat French sticks, jam and real-butter croissants for breakfast!

The French have a few more different eating habits you've probably never heard off such as, eating snails and eating frogs. Even I don't eating fancy those! They also dress differently and most people wear berets and carry a string of garlic around their neck. In the past Great Britain gave them Calais and in return France gave us the most sumptuous cheeses like Brie and Camembert. I've eaten Brie at home and it is absolutely divine.

Before we continued our journey to Holland my daddies showed me a big surprise: the vroom-vroom was jam-packed with lots of macaroons and Brie! I love travelling, I love France!

We travelled through France and Belgium before we arrived in Holland. Finally I could see the Holland House, it was like a Phoenix rising well above all the other houses. It was even bigger in reality. Wowzers, that was a massive house!

Daddy Michael parked the vroom-vroom car and I jumped through the open window onto the drive way where I was greeted by my grandparents Hendrick and Wil.
Granny Wil reached her arms out and came running towards me. "Hello handsome darling!", she said whilst she was showering me with kisses and cuddles.
Grand-pa Hendrick also joined in and gave me a massive hug and kisses. My grandparents were over the moon to see me. They gave me a present which I swiftly unwrapped with my paws and teeth ripping through the paper. Oh look! It's a new toy, a yellow lion! My tail was waggling. I looked up to my grandparents and hugged them to say thank you. Grand-pa gave me a little Dutch treat. It was a mini-doggy pancake! I love grand-dad and grand-ma, I love the Holland house, I love this country.
My daddies also hugged and kissed the grandparents and they gave each other a lot of gifts.
After we sat down for a cup of tea and a cup of coffee and telling the grand-parents about the smooth journey we've had they showed us all the rooms in the Holland House.
We walked up the stairs and the grandparents showed us their rooms on the first floor.
Their bedroom had a super-queen size bed, an en-suite bathroom and a balcony which overlooked the lake, the fields with tulips and the windmill.

They also showed us the room where my daddies would be sleeping. It looked like a wooden cabin which was called the beach hut, deep down inside the house. Amazing! It had a King-size bed, a coffee table and two leather chairs. From the top windows you could see outside the wheels of the vroom-vroom which was parked in front of the Holland-House.
I was allocated a room on the ground-floor with a super-King size bed! The room also had underfloor heating so yes indeed, I was a happy doggy!

We walked back up the stairs and grand-ma started making more tea and coffee in the open kitchen area. The Dutch do drink an awful lot of coffee and tea. Before Grand-dad Hendrick retired he used to work for the Dutch coffee company Douwe Egberts. The company still delivers to him every month a gift-box full of coffee and tea bags.
I sniffed the air and I could smell a lot of irresistible smells coming from the dinning table. Wow, that smelt good! I could tell that the table top was covered in yummy food! I could see warm pancakes staggered on a golden plate, a tub of clotted cream, real-butter, a pot of honey, jars of jam, a bowl with iced-sugar, treacle, grated Dutch cheese, ham and sliced pineapple! I could also see lemon-cakes, cubes of turkish delight and vanilla-muffins.
"Let's celebrate your arrival with a typical Dutch traditional meal", said grand-ma Wil, "I have made you a big pile of pancakes! You can help yourself to any topping you like. Take your seats and dig in before they get cold!" That was a big surprise! We all took our seats and were munching through all the pancakes. They were delicious. At the end of the meal all the pancakes were gone. My belly was full. I would have a good nights rest in my new room tonight.

It was time to bring my baggage into my room. My daddies and grand-parents helped me bring in my basket, my sheep cloth, my giraffe cushion, Big Ted, Lizzy the lizard, Teddy, Red rope, mini rope, bottle, Rudolph, my antler, my food and my water and the food bowls.
"Boys, was there any room left in the car for your luggage?" said grand-ma with a smile.
"There was just enough space left for our suitcases", said Daddy Richard, "they're still in the boot. We also brought over a little surprise from France: delicious Brie and macaroons!"
"How lovely", said grand-dad, "we can have that with a nice cup of coffee tonight!"

In the evening we played tug with the red rope and we all ran around the table with Rudolph and Lizzy the lizard until I was a very tired-bubbas. It was an amazing day, we drove 350 miles and we had the most delicious meal ever. My daddies picked me up and brought me to my room where they put me down on the super-King size bed. It was time to go to sleep and I would be dreaming of pancakes with grated cheese, ham and pineapple and macaroons.

The Summer-Holiday in Holland was absolutely great and thanks to the vroom-vroom we were able to meet the rest of our family. My daddies drove us and the grand-parents to grand-ma's sister Cornelia who lives in a house in a forest in the city of Arnhem.

The Tim-Tim guided us to aunty Cornelia's house which was right on the edge of the forest. Aunty Cornelia welcomed us with open arms and a lot of hugs and cuddles.

"Hello handsome!", she said, "OMG, you're so cute! Come in and make yourself comfortable on the sofa. I have biscuits in the oven for all of you. After everybody was seated Aunty Cornelia walked into the lounge with a big tray and she served out the cups of coffee and tea and the freshly baked biscuits. My biscuits were served on a special plate and I was also given a bowl of water. Yummy!

The family had a chat about how beautiful aunty's house was and how fortunate she was to live nearby this beautiful forest. Aunty Cornelia told us about the history of the forest. "Back in the 14th century there were nuns living in the enchanted forest at the bottom of the hills. They lived in a convent made out of grey bricks and next to the convent was a grave-yard. One day there was a storm and a very old oak tree was struck by lightning. The old oak tree fell on top of the convent and the grave yard leaving nothing but a pile of broken bricks and stones. Luckily all the nuns were on a pilgrimage trip to Italy and upon their return to the forest they were devastated to see that their convent had been smashed by the old oak tree. The nuns decided to leave the enchanted forest to build a new convent far away from any trees".

Aunty Cornelia continued: "Now, the story goes that hundreds and hundreds years later a majority of the members of the council voted to remove the oak in order to create a public pathway through the forest. One day the builders arrived to remove the old oak tree. When they successfully had lifted up the old oak tree with a crane they found one tomb stone underneath the tree which was still intact. The person named on the stone was Sister Clare Beak hence the park was given the name Clarenbeek. The mayor of Arnhem decided to erect the tomb stone at a special place in the forest in memory of Sister Clare. All people visiting the forest would be able to enjoy the wonderful views from where the stone was placed overlooking the valleys and hills of the forest", told Aunty Cornelia.

I had tears of joy in my eyes. What a beautiful story. Then suddenly somebody knocked on the door. Aunty Cornelia walked to the door and opened it.

In the door opening stood Aunty Cornelia's daughters Gwendoline and Sharona.

Two beautiful ladies. I ran towards the door and they gave me lots of cuddles and kisses. Sharona had brought her beagle Buffles to meet me. Yay! A new friend!

We decided to go out for a stroll through the hills and the valleys of the forest.

Buffles and I took the lead and we were chasing the rabbits, the squirrels and the birds.

I also saw a brown elegant looking horse galloping into the forest. Buffles and I were quite taken by this beautiful creature until it started to make very loud snorting horse-noises.

I wasn't sure about these horse noises so I barked at the horse and then I sprinted away into the woods.

I was followed by a running Buffles, grand-ma Wil, grand-dad Hendrick, Aunty Cornelia, Gwendoline, Sharona and my daddies. "Buster! Sit!", Daddy Michael suddenly said as he was running right behind me. I stopped, skidded over the path and came to a total stand-still. "Buster, sit!" I plonked my bum down on the path. "He's a good boy!", said Daddy Michael and he gave me a freshly made biscuit. He also gave one fresh biscuit to Buffles. Everybody gathered around us, totally out of breath, and by the looks of it they all could do with a break. "We're back to my house", said Aunty Cornelia, "it's just behind the chestnut trees!" Great! We all walked back to aunty's house for more cups of tea and coffee and biscuits before the vroom-vroom brought us back to the Holland-House.

Summer-Holidaying in Holland was fun! We met up with Daddy Richard's brother Koko, his partner Saskia, their daughters and Layla the brown Labrador. They took us to a children's farm which was situated in a massive open air nature reserve. There were a lot of play facilities for the Koko-daughters and lots of trees, shrubs and grass for me and Layla.

Layla was quite an old lady dog and was very protective of me when we met some unfriendly geese.

We had a fantastic day in the city of Amersfoort, the place where grand-dad Hendrick had been born. It's a buzzing place with lots of shoppers, tourists, people and dogs. I was allowed to have lunch with my daddies in the bistro at the town square. There's not much light in bistros so I was hiding under the table in case somebody would trip over me. After the lunch we went back into the town centre. The medieval city is very historical whilst at the same time it's bursting with modern life. Amersfoort even sells Van Gogh chips.
Van Gogh was a famous Dutch artist but I don't think he painted any chips but his relatives may have made them?

One afternoon we had a visit from Aunty Anya (the Grimm-mother) and her daughters, the Grimm-sisters Claudia and Ilona. They totally adored me, and I totally adored them! They were like three special aunties to me.

Another day we went shopping in Utrecht with Koko, his partner Saskia, their daughters and the grand-parents. My daddies are film fanatics and we decided to visit the Media Market, a Valhalla shop for everything that has to do with audio and vision. My daddies weren't sure whether I could go into the shop but Saskia who is very brave said "Don't worry just put Buster into a shopping trolley." Hey presto we walked into the shop with Saskia pushing the trolley. My daddies were not sure but brave girl Saskia knew what she was doing. All the people in the shop smiled at me at where all the films were kept. By the time we reached the till I was surrounded by dozens of films. We would be watching all the films back home in the UK on the big television screen. I would be barking at other dogs, big faces and speedy and noisy vroom-vrooms.

After all this excitement we sat down for lunch in the Three Herrings Street.
When Daddy Richard lived in Utrecht he used to work in the CD shop in the Three Herrings Street. The whole street was owned by two music-moguls called Mr H and Mr M.
Mr H created a street fully dedicated to music. There were speakers on every corner of the street so all the people could listen to music. He created a shop for classical music, a shop for POP music, a shop where they sold instruments and one shop was dedicated to sheet music. One day the music-moguls wanted to retire and they sold all their shops. Nowadays the whole road consists of restaurants. Now that sounds more like music to my ears!

The time had come to say goodbye to the grand-parents, uncle Koko, Aunty Saskia, their daughters, Layla and the Holland House. It was time say goodbye to the swans, the ducks, the geese, the herons and the fish who daily visited the lake next to the Holland House. My daddies packed up the boot with my basket, my sheep cloth, my giraffe cushion, Big Ted, Lizzy the lizard, Teddy, Red rope, mini rope, bottle, Rudolph, my antler, my lion, macaroons, Brie, my food and my water and food bowls. There was just enough space for my daddies's suitcases.

I was settled down in the back of the vroom-vroom seated on my cashmere cushions. Daddy Michael and Daddy Richard also took their seats and we were ready to drive back to the UK.

My daddies promised me that we would be doing lots of exciting things when we're back. We would be attending Jan and Ruth's wedding at the Hove band stand, dancing at Brighton Pride, I would start my driving lessons with Uncle David Brakes and go out for dog-group walks with Kelly and my friends in the South Downs.

Next year we will be going back to the Holland House to celebrate grand-dad Hendrick's and grand-ma's Wil's 50th wedding anniversary.

This sounds well exciting. I can't wait to go back next year and see of al my Dutch friends and relatives. I can't wait for my next adventures!

Once upon a time
the first miniature schnauzer
was born

When you get a handsome dog-breed like the Miniature Schnauzer, the dog with the biggest personality in the world, it could be very interesting to read about their origins.

The Miniature Schnauzer is a small breed dog of the Schnauzer type and the story goes that they originated in Germany where it has been known as far back as the 15th century. They are dogs with good guarding tendencies and for many centuries, these dogs were kept as herders, guardians, ratters and simply as companions. Eventually they were developed into Giant, Standard and Miniature Schnauzers . The literal translation of Schnauzer in English is 'snouter' and in my mother tong, Dutch, it would be translated as 'snuiter'. The term comes from the German word for 'snout' because of the dog's famous and distinctively bearded snout.

Schnauzer-like dogs appear in several art works of this early period. Some famous paintings and statues by the masters of the time document their existence as early as 1492. Dutch painter Rembrandt and German painter Albrecht Durer both have included Schnauzers in their paintings, and Lucas Cranach the Elder shows one in a tapestry called 'Crown of thorns' dated 1501.

In Mecklenburg, Germany, there is a statue dating from the 14th century of a hunter with a Schnauzer crouching at his feet. Another Schnauzer appears in statuary in "The Night Watchman," dated 1620, in Stuttgart, Germany. A Miniature Schnauzer also appeared in a painting by the 18th century English painter Sir Joshua Reynolds.

The word "Schnauzer" appeared in dog literature for the first time in 1842, when it was used as a synonym for Wire-haired Pinscher. The Wire-haired Pinscher was accepted as a pure, individual breed around 1850. The breed was variously designated as Rauhaar Pinscher (rough-haired terrier), Rattenfanger (rat catcher), and Schnauzer. The Standard Schnauzers were crossed with other breeds such as the Affenpinscher which it is thought resulted in the dog the Miniature Schnauzer. The earliest recorded Miniature Schnauzer dates back to 1888, and the first to be exhibited was in 1899. The Miniature Schnauzer was originally used for guarding herds and to hunt rats.

In 1928, the Miniature Schnauzer had reached the UK and quickly proved itself to be a very popular breed.

Miniatures were first registered with Standard Schnauzers up until 1932, when they were issued a separate register.

In 1935 the breed's name was altered to Affenschnauzer (Monkey Schnauzer) by the Kennel Club. After one year it was reverted back to it's original name Miniature Schnauzer after objections from The German Miniature Schnauzer Club.

Before describing the Miniature Schnauzer, I would like to tell you a little bit more about the Affenpinscher as they appear to have some things in common with the Miniature Schnauzer.

This breed is also from German origin and was given the name 'Affenpinscher' because their face looks a little bit like a monkey. 'Affe' means ape or monkey in German. They have a shaggy look and their fur is harsh. When the coat is clipped it can be softer and fluffier. I am sure the miniature schnauzers won't take any offence should you call them 'a little monkey'!

Affenpinschers have a distinct appearance that some associate with terriers. They are active, adventurous, curious, and stubborn, but they are also playful.

The breed is confident, lively, affectionate towards family members and they are very protective of their family. They can also be a little territorial when it comes to their toys and food. This loyal little dog enjoys being with its family. This small breed dog becomes bored easily so the training should be varied. The affenpinscher has a terrier-like personality.

The Affenpinscher was introduced to the UK in 1975.

The Miniature Schnauzers are recognised in four colours: solid black, black and silver, salt and pepper (white and grey) and white (not in the US).

Miniature Schnauzers have a very square-shaped build, measuring 13 to 14 inches (33 to 36 cm) tall and weighing 10 to 15 pounds (4.5 to 6.8 kg) for females and 11 to 18 pounds (5.0 to 8.2 kg) for males. They have a double coat, with wiry exterior fur and a soft undercoat. In show trim, the coat is kept short on the body, but the fur on the ears, legs, belly, and face is retained.

Miniature Schnauzers are non-moulting dogs and their shedding is minimal and generally unnoticeable. They are obviously famous for their grumpy looks. They have a rectangular head with the characteristic beard, moustache and eyebrows, natural forward-folding ears (when cropped, the ears point straight upward and come to a sharp point). Their tails are naturally thin and short. They will also have very straight, rigid front legs, and feet that are short and round with thick, black pads.

Docking of tails and cropping of ears has become a controversial practice, especially for non-working dogs, and is now illegal or restricted in a number of countries worldwide.

Character

Miniature Schnauzers are an observant, alert and energetic breed and obedient to command. A Miniature loves a lot of company and affection. They are friendly, intelligent and willing to please. They are easy to train, they tend to be excellent watchdogs with a good territorial instinct, but more inclined toward barking than biting.

They are highly playful dogs and love your company, a typical people dog. They are a type of dog that can not be left alone for long periods of time. If so, they can become bored and create their own way of having fun (e.g. chewing furniture). Whether you work, or just need to go away during the day or evening it is recommended to leave a miniature schnauzer by themselves for no longer than 3 - 4 hours.

Should you be around in your house all day they can decide to take a nap in a different area or you can gate them in a different room/area away from you.

Miniature Schnauzers can compete in dog agility trials, obedience and showmanship. Schnauzers have a high prey drive and they can be very interested in any birds (large or small), snakes and rodents.

Miniature Schnauzers needs

They need sufficient space to live in and they need regular exercise. They are often kept in small apartments where they do not get enough space to fulfil their exercise needs unless they are taken outside three times a day for a nice walk or a run.

Miniature Schnauzers are always hungry and they'll literally eat anything! They are prone to put on weight so it's recommended to stick to a proportioned diet, regular walks and exercise. The secret is to adjust the amount of food depending on the amount of treats you give them. My advice would be to weigh their food before serving out so you'll never overfeed them.

Socialising and training

Socialising with other people and especially other dogs is essential. I would recommend to start as early as possible. You can start socialising Miniature Schnauzers from 8 weeks and onwards (unless they have had their injections). The younger they get introduced to people and dogs the easier it will be later in their life. They are a boisterous breed but a first encounter with something totally new may back them off to start with. It's a good experience for your dog to expose them to traffic on busy roads so they can get used to by bicycles, cars, buses and lorries. You can go for a walk in the quiet countryside and encounter horses and birds or you can visit a town or city full of people who are moving around and lots of traffic. Introduce him or her to children, elderly people, wheelchair users, people with walking sticks and prams, people wearing hats, skateboarders etc.

These things are very normal for you and form part of our everyday life but for a puppy these things can be quite an experience.

It's inevitable that during your walks you're going to bump into people with their dogs. Use these encounters. It's worth asking the person who is walking the dog if it's OK to introduce them to each other. The Miniature Schnauzer gets very excited when they spot a dog whether it's nearby or miles away. Miniature Schnauzers love to meet their old friends for a good old sniff and a play session and they also love to make new friends wherever they go.

Dog-trainers are there to help and they can turn your potentially unruly dog into a truly well-behaved doggy! We used the Good citizen scheme from the Kennel Club as they were recommended by several people including the vet and the pet services company which we use.

Grooming

Miniature Schnauzers have a specific groom cut that is standard among the Schnauzer breed. Schnauzers require regular grooming either by clipping or hand-stripping (mostly seen in show dogs).

Many Miniature Schnauzers who are family pets have regular grooming sessions to have their hair clipped. Clipping can be done by yourself or you can get your dog clipped by a dog-groomer. Clipping is done with the use of mechanical clippers (or shaver) and it produces a soft and silky coat. Stripping removes the loose undercoat coat; it may be done by hand, called finger stripping, or plucking, or with a stripping knife. Either way, stripping is an intensive process and requires patience perseverance.
All Schnauzers, whether they are Miniatures, Standards, or Giants, usually sport a beard, allowing the hair around their snouts to grow out. Left unclipped or unstripped, the body hair will grow two to four inches (5 to 10 centimetres), and will often tangle into mats and curls unless regular grooming is undertaken.

Health

Miniature Schnauzers are prone to comedone syndrome, a condition that produces pus filled bumps, usually on their backs, which can be treated with a variety of methods.

Miniature Schnauzers should have their ears dried after swimming due to a risk of infection, especially those with uncropped ears; ear examinations should be part of the regular annual check up. Miniature Schnauzers are active all of their lives, full of energy and always excited! They can live for up to 15 years and are one of the longer-lived small dog breeds.

Miniatures Schnauzers always have an appetite for food and are prone to put on weight when they are not following a proportioned diet. Problems that may occur as a result of high fat levels are hyperlipidemia which may increase the possibility of pancreatitis. Other health issues found in Miniature Schnauzers are diabetes, bladder stones and they may experience issues with their eyes. Firstly hereditary and/or congenital cataracts and secondly retinal atrophy can occur although this is very rare.

Puppies can be tested for the congenital form at six to eight weeks and it's recommended that you only buy a puppy that has been tested. The Miniature Schnauzer's eyes should be examined annually.

Most breeders will get the dog's eyes tested by a vet registered under the British Veterinary Association or Kennel Club Eye Scheme.

Getting a Miniature Schnauzer

We got our Miniature Schnauzer through the Kennel Club in the UK. You can contact the Kennel Club or visit their website to enquire whether any members living in your area have puppies available. You can also contact the breeders directly and tell them what gender and colour you are looking for. If you go to a breeder as recommended by the club, you can meet the puppies and their mother. It's highly recommended to ask the breeder to see the mother and (if possible) the environment where the puppies live which should be clean and dry.

The breeder may ask whether you're going to use the dog as a company dog, as a show-dog or as a stud. Get as much advice on selecting the ideal puppy from experts about the breed and on how to raise them.

I would recommend to research the breeders and make contact with at least three breeders before making a choice. Some people advise to see as many breeders as possible. Always ask to the see eye testing certificates of the mother and sire. Please note that not all owners will have a copy of the sire's certificate but they should have made sure that he has an up to date certificate before mating, and all puppies should be litter screened before leaving for their new home.

Puppies should be bought when they are at least 8 weeks old. It's not recommended to buy a puppy under 7 weeks of age.

You should be given a diet sheet by your breeder and an example of the food the puppy has been having. The breeder should also recommend you to take the Miniature Schnauzer to your vet within one week after buying the puppy for a health check. If you have bought a pedigree through the Kennel Club the breeder will explain to you how you can change ownership of the Miniature Schnauzer.

You can buy books about raising and showing the Miniature Schnauzer or you could join the Miniature Schnauzer Club.

The Miniature Schnauzer Club operates a breed rescue service. These dogs intend to be older dogs and the advantage is that most of them already have been trained!

The Kennel Club

The aim of the Kennel Club's Assured Breeder Scheme is to promote good dog breeding practices and to help puppy owners find responsible breeders. The Kennel Club is the UK's largest organisation dedicated to protecting and promoting the health and welfare of all dogs. Besides being a voluntary register for pedigree dogs and crossbreed dogs, the Kennel Club offers dog owners and those working with dogs an unparalleled source of education, experience and advice on puppy buying, dog health, dog training and dog breeding.

The Kennel Club can be contacted as follows:

Website: www.thekennelclub.org.uk
Telephone: 01296 318540

Opening times: Monday - Friday 9:00 - 17:00, excluding Bank Holidays.

Good Citizen Dog Scheme
Email: gcds@thekennelclub.org.uk

Animal Doctor Clarissa's doggy-workshop

Looking after a pet is a massive responsibility. Dogs are friends, playmates for you and they also need a lot of care, attention and most of all ... love.

You need to show the grown-ups in your home that you are willing to help look after your pet and play with them.

Looking after your pet means you will need to help with:

Feeding
Cleaning
Exercise

You need the following items:

Bed (this could be a special bed or your own bed)
Collar, lead and tag
Food and water bowls
Dog food
Brush , comb, clippers and a pair of scissors
Treats, bones and chews
Poo bags
Toys
Caring For Your Dog

Animal Doctor

Once you have a pet I would suggest to visit the animal doctor, known as a vet, for a check up to make sure your dog is fit and healthy. Once a year your dog will need to have an injection to protect them from horrible diseases that would make your dog very poorly or they could possibly even die. The animal doctor will usually give your dog this injection at the same time as the check up. You can also have their teeth checked to ensure they are clean, strong and healthy.

Every month your dog should be protected against fleas and worms. The vet can give your dog a special treatment that will stop your dog from catching fleas and worms. If your dog is not treated, the fleas can give your dog itchy skin and the worms can give your dog an upset tummy.

Every week your dog should have his coat brushed. Some dogs like the miniature schnauzer ideally should be brushed daily. When your dog smells like big a puddle of mud it's time to give him or her a bath. Try to keep bathing sessions to an absolute minimum and you may need a grown-up to help you with this. Please use a lot of luke warm water to rinse their fur. Be careful that shampoo and water doesn't get into their ears and eyes.

Every day your dog needs to be fed healthy food. The animal doctor can tell you about the best food to feed your dog to help keep your dog fit and healthy and to keep your dog's teeth and coat in good condition. They also need to have fresh water all the time. Make sure they'll get plenty of exercise. A good walk together will be good exercise for you too, as well as being fun!

To help stop your dog from getting lost, the animal doctor can give your dog a special "tag" called a "microchip". The tag is injected under your dog's skin, at the back of the neck. If your dog does get lost, the microchip will have your details on it so that your dog can be returned to you. It will be compulsory for all dogs to be microchipped from 6 April 2016.

Every dog in the UK while on a public highway or place of public resort must wear a collar with the name and address of the owner inscribed on it or a plate or badge attached to it. You can buy them from pet shops, online and some animal doctors may sell them too. You will need the help from a grown-up to get this done for you.
If your dog is ever unwell, or if you would like to know more about looking after your dog, contact your local vet who will be pleased to help you.
Don't forget to play with your dog and most of all, give your dog lots of love!

Quiz-time!

Have you ever heard about mixed dog breeds? They are dogs which have two different parents for example a mini schnocker is a cross between a Miniature Schnauzer x Cocker Spaniel. Can you guess the parents of the following miniature schnauzer mixed breeds?

Bolonauzer
Miniature Schnauzer x Bolognese

Bowzer
Basset Hound x Miniature Schnauzer

Carnauzer
Cairn Terrier x Miniature Schnauzer

Chizer
Miniature Schnauzer x Chihuahua

Chonzer
Miniature Schnauzer x Bichon Frise

Miniature French Schnauzer
Miniature Schnauzer x French Bulldog

King Schnauzer
Cavalier King Charles Spaniel x Miniature Schnauzer

Mauzer
Maltese x Miniature Schnauzer

Miniature Schnoxie
Miniature Schnauzer x Dachshund

Miniboz
Miniature Schnauzer x Boston Terrier

Pom-A-Nauze
Miniature Schnauzer x Pomeranian

Schnau-Tzu
Shih Tzu x Miniature Schnauzer

Schneagle
Miniature Schnauzer x Beagle

Schnocker
Cocker Spaniel x Miniature Schnauzer

Schnoodle
Miniature Schnauzer x Poodle

Schnorgi
Miniature Schnauzer x Pembroke Welsh Corgi

Schnu
Shiba Inu x Miniature Schnauzer

Shnug
Pug x Miniature Schnauzer

Snorkie
Miniature Schnauzer x Yorkshire Terrier

Wauzer
Miniature Schnauzer x West Highland White Terrier

Miniature Schnauzer Rules

1. The Miniature Schnauzer is not allowed in the house.

2, The Miniature Schnauzer is allowed in the house, but only in certain rooms.

3. The Miniature Schnauzer is allowed in all the rooms, but has to stay off the furniture.

4. The Miniature Schnauzer is only allowed on the sofa-bed for the guests.

5. The Miniature Schnauzer is allowed on all the furniture, but is not allowed to sleep with the humans.

6. The Miniature Schnauzer is allowed on the bed, but only by invitation.

7. The Miniature Schnauzer can sleep on the bed whenever he wants, but not under the duvet cover.

8. The Miniature Schnauzer can sleep under the duvet cover every night.

9. Humans must ask permission to sleep under the duvet cover with the Miniature Schnauzer.

10. In all cases of disputes - the Miniature Schnauzer rules!

"Is he nice and comfy on the backseat Richard?", asks Michael.

Richard looks back over his shoulder to the backseat and said:

"Yes he looks very comfy and happy on his cushions. He is such a spoilt doggy!"

"Great. Let's start the car and turn the music on", said Michael, "we're off to ...".

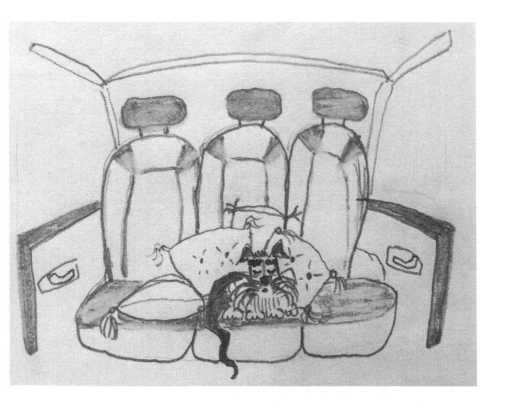

To be continued ...

Buster's pedigree name is Clarkmar's Top Gun.

Made in the USA
Charleston, SC
31 May 2016